RAINBOW magic ®

The Green Fairies

For the lovely
Milly Johnson – surprise!

Special thanks to
Sue Mongredien

ORCHARD BOOKS
338 Euston Road, London NW1 3BH
Orchard Books Australia
Level 17/207 Kent Street, Sydney, NSW 2000

A Paperback Original
First published in 2009 by Orchard Books.

A CIP catalogue record for this book is available
from the British Library.

ISBN 978 1 40830 480 8
10

Printed in Great Britain

The paper and board used in this paperback are natural recyclable
products made from wood grown in sustainable forests. The
manufacturing processes conform to the environmental regulations
of the country of origin.

Orchard Books is a division of Hachette Children's Books,
an Hachette UK company

www.hachette.co.uk

Milly
the River Fairy

by Daisy Meadows

ORCHARD

The fairies must be in a dream
If they think they can be called 'green'.
My goblin servants are definitely greenest
And I, of course, am by far the meanest.

Seven fairies out to save the Earth?
This idea fills me full of mirth
I'm sure the world has had enough
Of fairy magic and all that stuff.

So I'm going to steal the fairies' wands
And send them into human lands.
The fairies will think all is lost
Defeated again, by me, Jack Frost!

Contents

A Fairy Afloat

"Ooh, it's definitely colder than yesterday," Rachel Walker said, as she and her best friend Kirsty Tate strolled through Rainspell Park. "I can't believe we were so warm on the beach at the start of the week – and today we're all wrapped up in our woollies!"

Kirsty grinned at Rachel. "And *I* can't believe we were swimming in the sea with Coral the Reef Fairy a few days ago," she said in a low voice. "Imagine how freezing cold the water must be right now!"

Rachel shivered at the thought. "She'd have to use a *lot* of fairy magic to keep us warm today, wouldn't she?"

The two girls smiled at each other as they walked on through the park.

It was the autumn half-term, and they were both here on Rainspell Island for a week with their parents. Rainspell Island was the place where Kirsty and Rachel had first met. They'd shared a very magical summer together, and now this holiday was turning out to be every bit as magical! "Oh, I do love being friends with the fairies," Kirsty said happily, thinking about all the exciting adventures they'd had so far. "We really are the luckiest girls in the world, Rachel."

"Definitely," Rachel agreed. Golden-brown leaves were tumbling from the trees in the park every time the wind blew, and she noticed just then that some of the trees were already bare. "Well, it's certainly windy enough today to sail our boats, anyway," she said, as a yellow horse chestnut leaf floated down and landed at her feet.

She glanced at the paper boat she was holding. The girls had each made one back at their holiday cottage that morning. "They're going to whizz along with this breeze behind them."

"Here's the lake," Kirsty said as they rounded a corner and saw the stretch of blue water ahead of them. She held up her own paper boat and raised an eyebrow at Rachel. "Mine is going to be the fastest, you know."

Rachel laughed. "No chance!" she retorted.

The two girls had decorated their boats
with felt-tip pens and they were bright
and colourful. Kirsty's was red and gold,
and she'd written *Autumn Spirit*
along one side of it.
Rachel had
coloured hers
pink and lilac,
and had
called
it *Magical
Mist*. As they reached
the water's edge, both girls set their
boats carefully down on the surface,
and watched them float away. A gust
of wind blew them straight ahead, and
Kirsty and Rachel cheered as the boats
sailed quickly towards the middle of
the lake.

"Go, go, *Autumn Spirit*!" Kirsty cried.

"Let's run round to the other side of the lake so that we can catch them as they come in," Rachel suggested.

The girls sprinted along the path that circled the lake, making sure they checked on their boats every now and then. When the path rejoined the lakeside, the girls stopped expectantly, scanning the water to see where their boats had got to. Then Kirsty let out a cry of dismay. "Oh no, look, Rachel! There's a tyre sticking right out of the water – and our boats are heading straight for it. They'll get stuck there!"

Rachel opened her mouth to reply, but then noticed something else. Something very exciting! "Kirsty, have you seen who's standing on your boat?" she cried. "It's Milly the River Fairy!"

Kirsty looked at her boat, thrilled at the thought of another fairy adventure. Sure enough, there was Milly, one of seven fairies she and Rachel had met at the start of the week. Milly had long, honey-coloured hair, with a braid around the front, and wore a pretty blue-green top and a matching skirt, made of flowing, shimmering fabric.

Queen Titania and King Oberon had made seven fairies in training 'Green Fairies' for a trial period – with the special mission of helping humans look after the environment. Milly was one of the chosen Green Fairies, as well as six others called Nicole, Isabella, Edie, Coral, Lily and Carrie. Unfortunately, just as the new Green Fairies were about to be given their magic wands, wicked Jack Frost and his goblins had appeared and snatched them up.

"I'm sure my goblin servants will give a whole new meaning to the words *being green.*" Jack Frost had sneered. And with that, he and his goblins vanished into the human world, where they'd been causing all sorts of problems with the magic wands ever since.

Fortunately, Kirsty and Rachel had been able to help five of the fairies get back their stolen wands, but two of the wands were still missing – those belonging to Milly the River Fairy and Carrie the Ice Cap Fairy.

Milly was smiling and waving at them now from where she stood on Kirsty's boat. But Kirsty didn't smile back. "Oh no," she said, struck by a flash of fear. "I don't think Milly's seen that tyre – and the boat's going to crash into it any second. If it bumps too hard, the boat will sink!"

Sink or Swim?

Kirsty began waving her arms frantically above her head, trying to warn the little fairy. "Watch out!" she yelled. "Milly – get off the boat!"

But the wind was so strong it snatched Kirsty's words away, and Milly didn't seem to hear. She clearly thought Kirsty was just being friendly, and merely beamed and waved back at her.

"If Milly gets knocked in the water and her wings become wet, she won't be able to fly," Rachel realised in horror. "Milly! You're going to crash!" she yelled, waving like Kirsty.

It was no good. Milly went on waving and smiling back at them…until moments later, when Kirsty's boat hit the tyre with a bump. Then Rachel's boat blew straight into Kirsty's – and they both wobbled precariously.

"They're sinking!" Kirsty cried in
horror as she saw water splashing over
the edge of hers. It leaned to one
side…but luckily, just as it was about to
capsize, the girls saw Milly dart up into
the air, her wings fluttering
furiously as she zoomed
away from
the boats.

Down went the boats, their coloured sides becoming soggy within moments. Milly flew over to the girls, her face pale and drawn.

"Are you OK?" Rachel asked, seeing the little fairy shivering all over. "We were trying to warn you about that tyre but…"

Milly managed a smile. "Don't feel bad, it's not your fault," she said in a silvery voice. "That tyre should never have been in the lake in the first place. Since King Oberon and Queen Titania made me the fairy in charge of looking after rivers and waterways, I've been finding out just how bad water pollution is around the world.

I really need to find my wand so that I
can make the rivers and lakes cleaner."

Kirsty bit her lip. "And now our paper
boats have added to the litter in the
lake," she said, looking downcast. "I'm
really sorry, Milly, we didn't think."

Milly fluttered over to perch on Kirsty's
shoulder. "What's done is done," she said
kindly. "And it wasn't your fault the
boats crashed and sank. It's all the more
reason why I should get my wand back,
anyway!"

"Well, we'll certainly help you,"
Rachel said at once. She remembered
that King Oberon and Queen Titania
had promised that if the Green Fairies
were successful during their trial
period, they would be given the roles
permanently – which would be fantastic.

The more she and Kirsty learned about
environmental issues, the more it sounded
as if the world really needed some
dedicated Green Fairies to help clean
it up.

"Thanks," Milly said, smiling at
Rachel. "I've got an idea about where
my wand is, so with the small amount
of magic I have, I can take us all there
now, if you'd like."

"Of course," Kirsty said at once.
"There's nobody around to see us —
let's go!"

Milly sprinkled the girls with some
glittering turquoise fairy dust, which
made them shrink to her size,
and beautiful gauzy fairy
wings appeared on
their backs.

Milly threw another handful of fairy dust over them all, and Kirsty and Rachel found themselves surrounded by a sparkling golden whirlwind, that whisked them higher in the air.

Rachel managed to grab Kirsty's hand as they whizzed up in the golden mist, and clung on to her friend, breathless with excitement. Off on another fairy adventure – hurrah! And where would they find themselves this time?

Dirty Water

After a short time, Kirsty and Rachel felt their feet touch the ground once more, and the sparkly whirlwind cleared. They looked around and found that they were beside a wide river, which had grassy banks on either side. The water in the river was clear and blue, sparkling in the sunlight as it flowed along. Huge trees lined the riverbanks, their red and golden leaves casting bright reflections in the river.

"It's beautiful here," Rachel sighed. "Oh, look! Is that a deer?"

They all turned to see where Rachel was pointing. Kirsty held her breath as the deer emerged from between the trees. The creature was young and anxious-looking, her wide eyes checking this way and that for danger as she trotted towards the river. Her reddish-brown coat shone in the sun as she bent her head gracefully to drink from the water.

Elsewhere a group of squirrels were playing in a large beech tree, scampering up and down the trunk and

swinging from the branches like
miniature fluffy acrobats. Little pink and
white flowers grew in clumps around the
trees, and birds called to each other.
Kirsty and Rachel couldn't stop smiling
at the scene before them. It really seemed
like a perfect place!

Milly had tensed slightly and seemed to be listening for something. Then she smiled too. "My wand *is* near here, I can sense it," she said. "Come on, let's fly down the river and see if we can find it."

Rachel, Kirsty and Milly fluttered up in the air and followed the river. After a few minutes of flying they rounded a bend in the river, and the scene changed abruptly. Ahead stood a big factory with smoke pouring from its chimneys.

The sound of loud, rumbling machinery filled the air. Even worse, there was a dirty yellow froth on the surface of the water. "Ugh!" cried Rachel, wrinkling her nose. "Why does the river look like that?"

Milly gave a sigh. "The factory pumps
out its waste straight into it here," she
said sadly. "And that's a really bad thing:
the waste makes the water harmful to
drink, and the fish living in the river get
ill or die. The waste also kills some of
the plants that live in the river."

Kirsty felt upset hearing
this. "That's
awful," she
said, noticing
the way the
yellow
froth on
the water
clung to the
edge of the
grassy riverbank
as it splashed there.

And it smelled horrible too – a nasty, chemical sort of smell.

"Yes," Rachel agreed, then she put her hands on her hips. "Well, it makes it even more important for us to find Milly's wand and get it back for her, so that she can do something to clean up this river – and all the others like it."

"Yes," said Milly. "And—"Then she broke off. "Oh no," she cried, pointing ahead. "We've got to stop that deer. Hurry!"

She whizzed off at top speed, and
Kirsty and Rachel realised why: another
deer was heading towards this part of the
river. If she drank from the dirty water,
she might become ill. Milly waved her
hands and whispered some magical
words so that she would be able to talk
to the deer. Flapping their wings as hard
as they could, Kirsty and Rachel flew
after the little fairy.

"Don't drink that!" Milly called out, swooping towards the animal, who was just bending her head down to the water. "Please! It's polluted – really filthy and full of bad chemicals. It might make you poorly if you have any of it."

The deer raised her head and blinked her large brown eyes at the sight of Milly, and then Rachel and Kirsty fluttering in front of her. Then she gazed down at the water with a sad look on her face. "Thank you for the warning," she said. "My name's Dotty."

"I'm Milly, and this is Kirsty and Rachel," Milly said. "And there's some lovely clean water further upstream, once you get past this smelly factory. It'll be much nicer to drink than this."

Dotty smiled at her and bobbed her head. "Thank you," she said. "Usually I drink further down the river, but there are some very strange creatures there today, making a lot of noise. I was a bit scared of them, so thought I'd come here instead."

Rachel's ears pricked up at the deer's words. "What sort of strange creatures?" she asked.

Dotty gave a shudder. "Horrible shouty creatures," she said. "They're like little green men, and they're sailing on the river, frightening all the animals with their screaming and hollering."

"Little green men?" Kirsty echoed, her eyes lighting up. "I think we know who they are."

"Goblins!" chorused Rachel and Milly.

Racing Goblins

"Dotty, you're a star," Milly said,
patting the deer's black nose.

"I am?" Dotty asked, looking puzzled.

"You are," Kirsty smiled. "Thank you.
We've got to fly now. Goodbye!"

Kirsty, Rachel and Milly set off,
following the river again as it wound its
way through the woodland. They left
the factory behind, and the water
began to get clearer once more. It also
became much faster, Rachel noticed.

In fact, after a while, the current of the river looked so strong that the water was positively whizzing along below them,

splashing and bubbling as it tumbled over the rocky riverbed.

A short time later, they heard voices – high-pitched shrieks and excited cheers. "That's definitely the goblins," said Milly. "But what *are* they doing?"

It wasn't long before the three fairies found out. When they rounded the next bend of the river they saw four goblins racing along on home-made rafts, two on each one.

"And look what that goblin is holding," Milly hissed, pointing down at them. "My wand!"

Kirsty and Rachel saw that a goblin with a particularly hooked nose had a sparkly magic wand in his hand, which he was using to point in the direction in which they should sail.

"Straight on, boys!" they heard him shouting. "Wheeee! This is fun."

"Let's hide in this tree and make a plan," Milly suggested in a low voice. "The goblins don't know we've found them – we should keep it that way for as long as we can."

"Good thinking," Rachel said, as they perched in a line on a leafy branch. "If they don't know we're here, we can surprise them."

Kirsty nodded. "They're focussing so hard on racing that they're only looking ahead, and not up in the air," she noticed, leaning over slightly to watch the noisy goblins.

"So maybe if we dive straight down on them from above, we'll be able to catch them off guard and snatch the wand before they even know we're there."

"Yay!" Rachel cheered. "They won't know what's hit them."

Milly seemed to like the idea too. "As soon as I touch the wand, it'll shrink to its Fairyland size, so I'll easily be able to fly away with it," she said. "Let's do it!"

The three fairies set off, swooping high
above the goblins on their rafts. They'd
obviously built the rafts themselves out
of bits of rubbish, Kirsty realised. One
seemed to be made of planks tied
on to some big plastic
barrels, while another
was made of
wooden poles
which had been
tightly lashed
together. The
goblins were
using flat
pieces of
wood as paddles.

The hook-nosed goblin was holding
the wand in front of him. "That's it, lads,
keep going," he said bossily. "There's a

bend coming up, make sure you steer into it, remember."

The goblin sitting next to him rolled his eyes. "All right, all right, Captain Hook," he muttered under his breath.

The goblin with the wand scowled. "I told you not to call me that!" he snapped, forgetting, in his anger, to point the wand.

Kirsty and Rachel had to press their hands to their mouths to stop themselves giggling.

"I think this might be a good time to grab the wand," Milly hissed with a grin. "Here I go…"

Down she plunged, arms pointing in front of her as she flew. Kirsty and Rachel watched in excitement. This was actually going to be easy for once, Rachel thought with a smile.

But just as she was about to say as much to Kirsty, the rafts both knocked into a boulder in the middle of the river with a bump. The goblin holding the wand staggered, trying to regain his balance — and the wand went flying out of his hand!

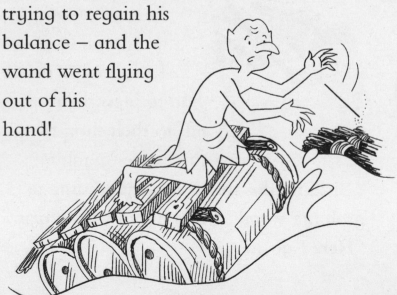

Milly made a dive for it but she was too late…and the wand landed in the water with a loud plop.

A look of horror spread over Milly's face. "The wand's floating away," she cried to Kirsty and Rachel. "Come on — we've got to find it before it's lost for ever. Follow that wand!"

Rafting Over Rapids

The goblins looked up in dismay as they heard Milly's shout. "Fairies? Yuck!" wailed a tall goblin. "They're after our wand, I bet. Well, we can't let them get it!"

"No way!" agreed a short, squat goblin with a mean face. "Jack Frost will be really angry if we lose it. Come on, paddle harder, guys, we've got to get that wand back!"

The goblins threw themselves whole-
heartedly into their paddling, and their
rafts whizzed along after the wand.

Overhead, the three fairies were
chasing after it, too. Fortunately, the
wand was quite easy to follow, as it left
behind a golden trail of sparkles, but the
fast current meant it rushed along with
the water very quickly.

"I think we should fly closer to the river," Rachel called to Milly and Kirsty. "That way we can grab the wand as soon as we get near it."

"Good thinking," Kirsty replied, and they swooped low over the water, so that they just skimmed it as they zoomed along.

It was really exciting, flying so fast,
but the three friends hadn't reckoned on
there being so much rubbish floating in
the river – empty bottles and plastic bags
– and it was hard work, having to dodge
around these obstacles.

"There's so much litter!" Rachel cried,
swerving quickly in order to avoid a
broken umbrella caught up against a
rock. Its spokes were sharp and pointed,
and her heart pounded as
she just managed
to miss it.

"I know, it's
disgusting," Kirsty
said, flying over yet
another
wrinkled
plastic bag.

"We've got to get to that wand before the goblins do. This river needs a serious clean-up."

"Oh, help!" Milly suddenly said nervously. "Have you seen what's ahead? Rapids!"

Kirsty and Rachel gulped as they saw what she meant. The river was now flowing more steeply downhill, causing the water to turn white and foamy as it churned over the rocks.

The goblins looked anxious, too. Their rafts were bobbing up and down wildly with the strong current, and the tall goblin in particular was looking very seasick, his eyes closed, as he clung on to the raft.

Just then, the magic wand was flipped up on its end by the bubbling water, so that it was carried along with its tip in the air. "Quick!" cried Kirsty, soaring towards it. She grabbed hold of it, as did Rachel, and together, they pulled it free of the water.

"Yes!" Kirsty cried. "We've got it, Milly!"

Milly let out a cheer, but then, just as she was flying over to grab it, the goblins on the barrel-raft whizzed by, and snatched the wand clean out of Rachel and Kirsty's fingers!

"Hey!" Rachel yelled. "Give that back!"

"Not likely," jeered the hook-nosed goblin, twirling it between his fingers. "I'm hanging on to this now…whoah!"

His raft was bumping and bouncing even harder on the current, and the goblin fell sideways. With a shout of fear, he reached for a nearby rope to hold on to — and as he did so, the wand slipped from his fingers and splashed down into the water again.

"You idiot," the short goblin bellowed, shaking his fist. "You can't be trusted with anything!"

"I'm not an idiot," the hook-nosed goblin raged back. "You're the idiot, suggesting making these rafts in the first place. This is all *your* fault."

The short goblin was just about to shout a reply when he glanced ahead – and then gave a yell of terror. "Waterfall!" he screamed. "Help!"

Down the Waterfall

The two rafts plunged over the waterfall, and the goblins fell off immediately, wailing and shrieking as they hurtled through the air. The wand was falling too, and, as she and her friends flew down past the roaring waterfall, sharp-eyed Rachel managed to fly over and grab it deftly in midair. It was heavy for a little fairy, though, and the weight of the wand pulled her down sharply.

"Milly!" she called above the noise of the water as it crashed below them. "Here!"

Milly zoomed over at once, her hand outstretched, and grabbed hold of the wand. As soon as Milly touched it, the wand shrank down to fairy-size, and Rachel was able to fly a safe distance above the rushing waterfall again. "Phew!" she sighed in relief.

Meanwhile, Milly was waving the
wand in the goblins' direction, muttering
some magic words. A stream of turquoise
sparkles shot from the wand and swirled
around the goblins…just in time to make
them land on their rafts
again at the bottom
of the waterfall.

"Now to guide them safely to the shore," Milly said, with another flourish of her wand. Once again, a flurry of turquoise sparkles flooded out from it, and the two rafts were magically steered to the river bank. The goblins clambered onto land with

shaky legs. All four of them looked wet through and utterly miserable.

"I think you'd better go back to Jack Frost's castle now and dry off," Milly called sweetly, hovering above them with Rachel and Kirsty on either side of her.

The goblins all glared, but said nothing. They knew when they were beaten, and trudged away, heads down, bickering amongst themselves.

Milly flung her arms around Rachel and Kirsty. "Thank you, girls!" she cried. "Thank you for everything. I don't think I've ever flown quite so fast in my life."

Kirsty beamed. "That was really exciting," she said. "Glad we could help."

Milly eyed the river and then her wand. "Now…I've got work to do, haven't I?" she said. "Come on!"

The three of them flew up to the top of the waterfall again, and back to where the water was still littered and polluted from the factory waste.

Milly waved her wand over the river and, as she did so, the dirty froth vanished from the surface and the plastic bags and other items of litter disappeared. Kirsty and Rachel cheered, but Milly still looked troubled. "Well, it's clean for the time being, but it's up to you humans now.

You must stop factories from dumping waste in the river, and put rubbish in recycling bins and dustbins, rather than here."

"You're right," Rachel said. "We've got to work together."

"There's Dotty again," Kirsty said, suddenly noticing the pretty deer they'd met earlier. "Let's tell her the good news."

They flew over to greet Dotty, who promptly drank from the clean water. "Delicious," she said. "Thank you!"

"My pleasure," Milly replied. "And now I should go. I've got plenty of other rivers to clean up, after all. Goodbye, Kirsty! Goodbye, Rachel! Thanks again."

The three friends hugged each other, and then Milly waved her wand. Kirsty and Rachel were whisked up in the sparkly whirlwind once more and went whizzing away at top speed.

Moments later, the two girls were back at Rainspell Lake – and the first thing they noticed was that the tyre had vanished from where they'd seen it earlier. "Milly is a quick worker," Rachel laughed happily. "Isn't fairy magic amazing?"

"But we've got to do our bit too, as she said," Kirsty reminded her. "Maybe we could write to some of the local factories and ask them to help keep rivers and lakes clean."

"That's a great idea," Rachel agreed. "And maybe we could…oh! Look, Kirsty!"

Rachel was pointing to a clump of reeds near the water. Kirsty's eyes widened as she saw what had been hidden inside. "It's our boats!" she squealed, leaning over and pulling them out. "Oh, and look, they're good as new again!"

Both girls examined their boats in delight. The paper was now smooth and dry, and the colours fresh and bright, as if they'd only just been drawn on. And, thanks to Milly's magic, no doubt, there were now a few fairy passengers drawn on the inside of the boats, all beaming up at Kirsty and Rachel.

"I'm going to keep this for ever," Rachel declared happily. "What a brilliant surprise!"

Rachel linked an arm through Kirsty's and the two girls headed back towards their holiday cottage.

"It's our last day here tomorrow," Kirsty said, suddenly remembering. "And we still need to find Carrie the Snow Cap Fairy's wand."

"I really hope we can," Rachel said. "The world already looks so much better for having the Green Fairies."

Just then, carried on the breeze, the girls both heard a tiny, faint tinkling sound, almost as if Fairyland bells were ringing. The girls looked at one another and grinned. "Sounds like the fairies agree with you too," Kirsty said. "We really *must* help Carrie find her wand tomorrow!"

Now it's time for Kirsty and Rachel
to help...

Carrie the Snow Cap Fairy

Read on for a sneak peek...

"Brr!" Shivering, Rachel Walker glanced across the bedroom at her best friend, Kirsty Tate, who was just waking up too. "It's really cold this morning, isn't it?"

Kirsty yawned and nodded. "It's freezing," she agreed. "It's been getting colder all week."

"Well, I suppose it   the end of October," said Rachel. She sat up in bed, wrapping the duvet around her shoulders. "It'll be winter soon – but I didn't expect the weather to change quite so fast!"

"Haven't we had a lovely holiday

though, Rachel?" Kirsty sighed happily. "It's been so special to come back to Rainspell Island, where we first met."

The Walkers and the Tates were spending the autumn half-term holiday together in a pretty little cottage on beautiful, magical Rainspell Island.

"Yes, it's been brilliant!" Rachel smiled. "And we're even having another fairy adventure, just like we did the first time we visited Rainspell."

"Only this time it was *our* turn to ask the fairies for help," Kirsty pointed out.

When Kirsty and Rachel had returned to Rainspell Island a week ago, they'd been horrified to see the wide, golden beach covered in litter. So they'd asked the king and queen of Fairyland if their fairy friends could help them to clean up the human environment.

The king and queen had explained to the girls that fairy magic could only do so much, and that humans had to help the environment too. But they had agreed that the seven fairies who were about to complete their training could become the Green Fairies for a trial period. The Green Fairies would work together with Rachel and Kirsty to try to make the world a cleaner place. If the fairies completed their training successfully, they would become permanent.

But just as the Green Fairies were about to be presented with their new wands, Jack Frost and his goblins had zoomed towards them on a ice bolt...

Read Carrie the Snow Cap Fairy to find out
what adventures are in store for Kirsty and Rachel!

Meet the
Green Fairies

Jack Frost's goblins make a mess everywhere they
go. Can Kirsty and Rachel clean things up
before the natural world is seriously harmed?

www.rainbowmagicbooks.co.uk

RAINBOW magic®

Meet the fairies, play games
and get sneak peeks at
the latest books!

www.rainbowmagicbooks.co.uk

There's fairy fun for everyone on
our wonderful website.
You'll find great activities, competitions, stories and
fairy profiles, and also a special newsletter.

Get 30% off all Rainbow Magic books at
www.rainbowmagicbooks.co.uk

Enter the code RAINBOW at the checkout.
Offer ends 31 December 2013.

Offer valid in United Kingdom and Republic of Ireland only.

Win Rainbow Magic Goodies!

There are lots of Rainbow Magic fairies, and we want to know which one is your favourite! Send us a picture of her and tell us in thirty words why she is your favourite and why you like Rainbow Magic books. Each month we will put the entries into a draw and select one winner to receive a Rainbow Magic Sparkly T-shirt and Goody Bag!

Send your entry on a postcard to Rainbow Magic Competition, Orchard Books, 338 Euston Road, London NW1 3BH.
Australian readers should email: childrens.books@hachette.com.au
New Zealand readers should write to Rainbow Magic Competition, 4 Whetu Place, Mairangi Bay, Auckland NZ.
Don't forget to include your name and address.
Only one entry per child.

Good luck!

Meet the
Ocean Fairies

Naughty goblins have smashed the magical conch
shell! Kirsty and Rachel must restore it
so that the oceans can have harmony again.

www.rainbowmagicbooks.co.uk